NO MORE CATS!

BY DARLENE WELTON
ILLUSTRATED BY MARIA GIBSON

Darlene Welton
Cheers! :)

Credit
River
Critters

Text by Darlene Welton
Illustrations by Maria Gibson
© Copyright 2016 Credit River Critters

No part of this publication may be reproduced in any form without the
permission of the publisher in writing.

Cataloguing data available from Library and Archives Canada

Design, layout and typography by Allen Zuk

Published worldwide by Credit River Critters

www.creditrivercritters.ca

Print ISBN: 978-0-9949425-0-0
Ebook ISBN: 978-0-9949425-1-7

for David

ECHO   POLLY   RUFUS

Mr. and Mrs. Brown lived in an enchanting house on the banks of the Credit River. They loved how the river sparkled in the sunshine and how the green grasses waved in the wind. They loved to sit and hold hands on the back porch and watch the red and golden sunrises and sunsets. But something was missing.

One day, Mrs. Brown turned to Mr. Brown and said, "I've figured it out: we need a pet! But not just any pet — one who needs a forever home." Mr. Brown with his big smile and twinkly blue eyes nodded in agreement.

So Mrs. Brown went to the Humane Society. She found two Siamese kittens curled up next to each other. They were sisters and had eyes as blue as the ocean, just like Mr. Brown's! One was silver and shy, but very playful. She liked to stay by her sister's side. The other was tiny, brown, and brave. She went right up to Mrs. Brown, but made sure her sister was close. Mrs. Brown fell in love with the sisters but couldn't decide which kitten to pick.

Mrs. Brown told Mr. Brown about the sister kittens. Mr. Brown knew the kittens would be sad if they had to be apart. He did not want to separate them just because Mr. and Mrs. Brown had only planned to take one. So Mr. Brown agreed that yes, there was enough space and love in their home for two sisters who were the best of friends. They named the kittens Polly and Echo.

The Browns and their two kitties were happy in their little house on the banks of the Credit River, but Mr. Brown said . . .

"Mrs. Brown,

NO
MORE
CATS!"

In the fall, Mrs. Brown heard about a gigantic cat named Rufus that nobody wanted. His paws were as big as oven mitts! Each paw had extra toes on it. Rufus had a medical condition called palsy which made him shaky. It made him zig and zag every time he walked. It made him tired. But Rufus couldn't help it. He just wanted to laze around on the sofa with someone he loved.

Mrs. Brown told Mr. Brown about Rufus. Mr. Brown knew that everyone had problems they could not help. He did not want Rufus to be alone just because he had trouble walking. So Mr. Brown agreed that yes, they had enough space and enough love in their home for a big, somewhat lazy zigzagging kitty named Rufus.

The Browns and their three kitties were happy in their little house on the banks of the Credit River, but Mr. Brown said . . .

"Mrs. Brown,

NO
MORE
CATS!"

Winter came and brought a wicked snowstorm. Mrs. Brown looked out her window and saw a poor mother cat trying to shelter her two kittens from the freezing cold. She coaxed the family onto the back porch. It was safe, cozy, and warm there. The little family stayed with the Browns all winter, and soon they were happy and healthy.

When spring arrived, Mr. and Mrs. Brown released the mother cat back into the wild. She missed being out on her own and was happy to be outside again. But the kittens were still small. They needed homes. Mrs. Brown found a nice family for the friendly boy kitten, but the girl kitten was afraid of humans. She only trusted Mr. and Mrs. Brown because they had saved her.

The Browns did not want the kitten to be alone just because she was afraid. So Mr. and Mrs. Brown agreed yes, they had enough space and enough love in their home for a half-wild kitty. They named her Bella.

The Browns and their four kitties were happy in their little house on the banks of the Credit River, but Mr. Brown said . . .

"Mrs. Brown,

NO
MORE
CATS!"

Summer came and Mrs. Brown heard about an elderly lady who needed to move from her home into a condo. Her name was Mrs. Grady. Mrs. Grady has two cats named Ellie and Lila. But pets were not allowed in the new condo. Mrs. Grady was heartbroken. She tried to find a new home for Ellie and Lila, but they were very old and no one wanted them.

Mrs. Brown went to visit Mrs. Grady and her old cats. Ellie was pure white. She looked like a polar bear and acted like a lioness, but purred and purred when humans were around. Lila was pure black and looked like a panther. She kept to herself but loved to play with toy mice all day long.

Mrs. Brown told Mr. Brown about the old kitties in desperate need of a loving home. He did not want them to be homeless just because they were old. He agreed that yes, they had enough space and enough love in their home for two old cats.

The Browns and their six kitties were happy in their little house on the banks of the Credit River, but Mr. Brown said . . .

"Mrs. Brown,
NO
MORE
CATS!"

Another fall arrived and Mr. Brown heard about an abandoned dog named Boomer. Boomer's family thought he was too much of a handful. He was brownish with soft, floppy ears. He loved to meet new people and lick their faces all over.

Mr. Brown told Mrs. Brown about the brownish dog in need of a home. Mrs. Brown did not want the dog to be alone just because he was energetic. She agreed that yes, they had enough space and enough love in their home for an unwanted, floppy-eared dog named Boomer.

The Browns, their six kitties, and their dog were happy in their little house on the banks of the Credit River, but this time Mrs. Brown said . . .

"Mr. Brown,

NO
MORE
DOGS!"

And so Mr. and Mrs. Brown and their six cats and one floppy-eared dog lived happily ever after in their little house on the banks of the Credit River.

CPSIA information can be obtained
at www.ICGtesting.com
Printed in the USA
BVHW021947050320
574245BV00005B/11